Welcome to ALADDIN QUIX

If you are looking for [...] with colorful character[...] [frie]ndly humor, easy-to-follow action, entertaining story lines, and lively illustrations, then **ALADDIN QUIX** is for you!

But wait, there's more!

If you're also looking for stories with tables of contents; word lists; about-the-book questions; 64, 80, or 96 pages; short chapters; short paragraphs; and large fonts, then **ALADDIN QUIX** is *definitely* for you!

ALADDIN QUIX: The next step between ready to reads and longer, more challenging chapter books, for readers five to eight years old.

Read all the ALADDIN QUIX books!

By Stephanie Calmenson

Our Principal Is a Frog!
Our Principal Is a Wolf!
Our Principal's in His Underwear!

Royal Sweets
By Helen Perelman

Book 1: *A Royal Rescue*
Book 2: *Sugar Secrets*
Book 3: *Stolen Jewels*

A Miss Mallard Mystery
By Robert Quackenbush

Dig to Disaster
Texas Trail to Calamity
Express Train to Trouble
Stairway to Doom
Bicycle to Treachery
Gondola to Danger

ROYAL SWEETS

Stolen Jewels

By Helen Perelman

Illustrated by Olivia Chin Mueller

ALADDIN QUIX

New York   London   Toronto   Sydney   New Delhi

To Karen Perelman, a royal jewel
—H. P.

ALADDIN QUIX
Simon & Schuster Children's Publishing Division
1230 Avenue of the Americas, New York, New York 10020
First Aladdin QUIX paperback edition January 2019
Text copyright © 2019 by Helen Perelman
Illustrations copyright © 2019 by Olivia Chin Mueller
Also available in an Aladdin QUIX hardcover edition.
All rights reserved, including the right of reproduction in whole or in part in any form.
ALADDIN and the related marks and colophon
are trademarks of Simon & Schuster, Inc.
For information about special discounts for bulk
purchases, please contact Simon & Schuster Special Sales
at 1-866-506-1949 or business@simonandschuster.com.
The Simon & Schuster Speakers Bureau can bring authors to your live event. For more information or to book an event contact the Simon & Schuster Speakers Bureau at 1-866-248-3049 or visit our website at www.simonspeakers.com.
Series designed by Jessica Handelman
Cover designed by Tiara Iandiorio
Interior designed by Heather Palisi and Jessica Handelman
The illustrations for this book were rendered digitally.
The text of this book was set in Archer Medium.
Manufactured in the United States of America 1218 OFF
2 4 6 8 10 9 7 5 3 1
Library of Congress Control Number 2018956783
ISBN 978-1-4814-9484-7 (hc)
ISBN 978-1-4814-9483-0 (pbk)
ISBN 978-1-4814-9485-4 (eBook)

Cast of Characters

Lady Cherry: Teacher at Royal Fairy Academy

Prince Frosting: One of Princess Mini's cousins from Cake Kingdom

Princess Cupcake: Prince Frosting's twin

Princess Mini: Royal fairy princess of Candy Kingdom

Princess Taffy: Princess Mini's best friend

Queen Swirl: Princess Mini's grandmother

Princess Swirlie: Princess Cupcake's best friend

Queen Sugarella: Queen of Candy Kingdom one hundred years ago

Gobo: Troll living in Sugar Valley

Butterscotch: Mini's unicorn

Bibi: Gobo's great-great-great-grandfather

Beanie: Royal chef

Princess Lolli and Prince Scoop: Princess Mini's parents and ruling fairies of Candy Kingdom

Chip: Palace guard

Lord Licorice: Music teacher

Contents

1

Class Trip

"Lady Cherry, where is our class going?" **Prince Frosting** asked our teacher. He was my cousin and in my first-year class at Royal Fairy Academy.

"Oh, I hope it is someplace

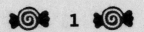

super sweet!" **Princess Cupcake** said. She was Frosting's twin sister. They were as different as fruit chews and lemon drops.

Lady Cherry clapped her hands. "I am going to write a clue on the board," she told the students.

I looked and saw . . .

Colorful jewels!

"Are we going to Sour Forest?" Prince Frosting asked, flying out of his seat. He always forgot to raise his hand before speaking.

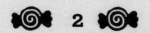 2

Lady Cherry gave Prince Frosting a stern look. "Please stay in your seat and remember to raise your hand," she said. "No, not Sour Forest." She looked around the room.

I thought I knew the answer. My parents were the ruling fairy princess and prince of Candy Kingdom. They had told me about a new royal crown jewels **exhibit** at the Chocolate Museum. I raised my hand.

"Princess Mini," Lady Cherry said, nodding at me, "what is your guess?"

"The royal crown jewels at the Chocolate Museum?" I asked.

"Yes, Mini! That's correct,"

Lady Cherry happily exclaimed.

"Oh, I always wanted to see those jewels," **Princess Taffy** said. "Don't they belong to Princess Mini's grandmother **Queen Swirl**?"

I smiled at Taffy. She was my best friend and the sweetest Candy Fairy I knew.

"The crown jewels are **sugar-tastic**!" I said. "I saw them last year at my grandfather's birthday party."

"The crown is kept in Queen Swirl's **vault** on Ice Cream Isles,"

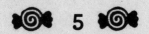

Lady Cherry said. "Queen Swirl only wears the crown for certain ceremonies."

"But the jewels don't *really* belong to her," Princess Cupcake said.

Taffy leaned closer to me. "She's just jealous that Queen Swirl isn't

from her side of the family," she whispered.

"Even though we're not related, I am named after the queen," **Princess Swirlie** said. She was Cupcake's best friend. "My parents lived on Ice Cream Isles before moving to Sugar Valley."

"Have you ever seen the special royal crown?" Cupcake asked.

Swirlie shrugged. "No," she said. **"But I want to!"**

2

Queen Sugarella

Lady Cherry smiled broadly. "Class," she announced. "We are *all* going to see the crown."

The whole class cheered.

Our teacher continued, "The jewels were a special gift to

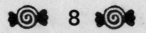

Queen Sugarella, who was the queen of Ice Cream Isles one hundred years ago."

"Whoa," Prince Frosting said.

"The Royal Crown Ball is tomorrow night at the Chocolate Museum," I said. "My grandmother is coming to Sugar Valley for the festivities."

"We will see the crown tomorrow *before* the ball," Lady Cherry said. Then she pulled down a map at the front of the classroom.

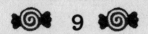

With a long sugarcoated licorice pointer, she circled Ice Cream
Isles on the map.

"Queen Sugarella once ruled
over Ice Cream Isles *and* Sugar
Valley. She kept the trolls safe,"
she told us.

Princess Cupcake wrinkled her nose. **"Ewww, trolls!** They steal Candy Fairy candy!" she screamed.

"Not *all* trolls," I said. I turned to Taffy and Frosting. The three of us had made friends with a troll named **Gobo** who lived in Chocolate Woods.

Many Candy Fairies were afraid of trolls, but the three of us were special friends with Gobo.

"Sadly, there was a time when trolls were known to take candy,"

Lady Cherry said. She frowned.

"But things are better now," I added.

Lady Cherry nodded. "Yes," she said. "Sugar Valley is a peaceful place."

I wondered if Gobo knew about Queen Sugarella and the trolls. **Sure as sugar**, I was going to find out!

3

Bibi's Gift

"**Come on!** Frosting called as he flew to the school courtyard.

Taffy and I had a made a plan with Frosting to meet after school. We wanted to visit Gobo.

As usual, we didn't tell Cupcake

or Swirlie we were going to Chocolate Woods. We didn't want them to know about our secret friend. Telling those two would be telling all Sugar Valley.

When the three of us were on my unicorn **Butterscotch**'s back, Frosting cheered. "I can't wait to talk to Gobo," he said.

"I wonder if Gobo knows about the **celebration**," I said. "Everyone is talking about the one-hundreth anniversary!"

"I took a book from the library about the crown jewels," Taffy said. She pulled the book from her bag.

I smiled at Taffy. She loved books almost as much as she loved jelly beans!

When we landed near Chocolate River, I put out my mini chocolate chips on the chocolate sand. Every

Candy Fairy has a special talent to make candy, and mine was making tiny chocolate chips. **Gobo loved them!**

"Here he comes," Taffy said. She pointed to the bushes.

"Hi!" Gobo called. "What's new?"

"We're going on a class trip," Taffy told him. "We're going to see the royal crown jewels at the Chocolate Museum."

"The jewels? The *crown jewels*? My great-great-great-grandfather

Bibi gave those to Queen Sugarella," Gobo said excitedly. He licked the chocolate off his fingers. "These chips are so good!"

"Hot Cocoa!" I exclaimed. "A *troll* gave the queen the crown jewels? I never knew that!"

"You are related to a famous troll!" Frosting exclaimed.

"Famous?" Gobo asked.

Taffy held up her book. "See?" she said. "He's written about in this history book."

"I know all about that story. Grandfather Bibi searched the Sugar Caves for the **perfect jewels**," Gobo said. "Then he put them in a crown."

"How did your grandfather cross the Sugar Seas?" Frosting asked. "That must have been a

dangerous ride for a troll."

Gobo picked up a stick. In the sand, he drew a small boat. "Bibi built a boat," he said.

"He was *very* brave," I said. "The Sugar Seas were rough waters. I wondered why Bibi made the trip."

4

Rough Waters

Taffy turned some pages in the book. "That part of the story isn't mentioned," she said. "There is only a chapter about the trolls leaving Ice Cream Isles."

She read aloud, "'The cold

weather made many of the trolls sick, so many left for Sugar Valley.'"

"That is true," Gobo said. "But Queen Sugarella was the one who planned the trip. Bibi returned later. He gave the queen the jewels as a thank-you gift for saving his life and the lives of many other trolls."

"I wonder why that part of the story isn't in the book," I said. **"Bibi should be celebrated too!"**

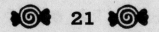

Gobo shrugged. "There were some bitter years when trolls stole candy crops in Sugar Valley," he said. "Many Candy Fairies are still afraid of trolls."

"I might just be a first year at Royal Fairy Academy," I said, standing up. "But I want to make sure things change—just like Queen Sugarella!"

Gobo smiled at me. "You look a little like Queen Sugarella," he said, pointing to the picture in Taffy's book.

"Thank you," I said. I felt my face get as hot as a **spicy** red candy.

"Look at those beautiful jewels," Taffy said. She flipped through her book and found a picture of the crown.

We all **huddled** together.

"I wish I could see the crown," Gobo said. He lowered his head. He looked so sad!

At that moment, I had the most **choc-o-rific** idea!

"Gobo, you should come to the ball tomorrow night!" I exclaimed.

"Me?" Gobo asked.

"Yes, you," I said. "You need to tell the Candy Fairies about Bibi."

"Um," Frosting said, poking my side, "then everyone will know about Gobo."

"Even Cupcake," Taffy added.

I knew if Gobo came to the ball, our friendship wouldn't be a secret anymore. But Sugarella had done so much for the trolls. Maybe I could too.

"It is time for you to tell Bibi's story," I said. "And for you to meet my parents and Candy Fairies in Sugar Valley."

"I can't do that!" Gobo cried.

And in a flash, he was gone!

5

Change of Plans

"Gobo!" I called. "Please come back!"

I didn't see him. Trolls have a special talent for disappearing quickly.

"Gobo!" I called again.

I flew up in the air and searched around the forest calling his name. I couldn't see him anywhere.

I landed next to Taffy and Frosting. Taffy shook her head. "He is gone," she said. "He looked really scared."

 27

"**Licorice laces**, he sure took off fast," Frosting added.

"I scared him," I said. I sat down on a chocolate tree **stump**. "I should have known better."

"Gobo is shy," Taffy said. "He probably doesn't want to go to a big Candy Fairy party."

"Maybe you need to explain there will be lots of candy and food," Frosting told me. "That is the best part of a ball!"

"No," I answered. "I think Gobo is afraid of Candy Fairies."

I plucked a chocolate chew from a bush and took a bite.

"But *we* are Candy Fairies," Frosting said.

"Exactly!" I said. "And he shouldn't be afraid. He has to tell everyone about Bibi."

Frosting stood next to me. "How are you going to make that happen?"

"I am not sure," I said. I reached for Taffy's book about the crown jewels, and I opened it to the page with Queen Sugarella and Bibi.

Frosting looked over my shoulder. "They seem like good friends," he said.

I nodded. "And we are good friends with Gobo," I replied.

"We *are* good friends," Gobo said quietly. He stuck his head

out from under a small bush.

My wings started to flutter. "Come sit with us, Gobo," I said. "Please?"

I held my breath. I hoped Gobo would come out of hiding.

6

An Invitation

"Will you please come to the party?" I asked Gobo.

"No one would want me there," he said sadly. He sunk his head into his hands.

"That is not true!" I told

him. "The three of us do!"

Frosting put a hand on Gobo's back. "We will be right there with you," he said. "I even have a suit you can wear."

Gobo grinned. "Really?"

"Sure," Frosting said. "I have one from when I was . . . shorter," he added, smiling.

I was happy Frosting was making Gobo feel more comfortable.

"I don't love the wearing a suit part," Frosting told Gobo. "The best part of the ball is the candy."

"Sure as sugar!" Taffy said. "And this celebration will definitely have the yummiest of treats!"

"**Beanie**, the castle chef, makes

the most **scrumptious** ones!" I said.

Gobo lifted his head. "Hmmm," he mumbled.

Maybe we were helping Gobo change his mind!

"We really want you to come," I said to Gobo. "I am going now to talk to my parents, **Princess Lolli** and **Prince Scoop**."

"And we will bring you an official invitation and Frosting's suit," Taffy said.

"Maybe," Gobo said.

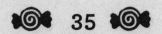

He still looked nervous.

My friends and I flew back to Candy Castle and rushed inside.

When we arrived, my parents were in the throne room. This was where they met with royalty and other visitors. **Chip**, one of the castle guards, was at the door.

"I am sorry Princess Mini," Chip said. "Your parents asked not to be **interrupted**."

"Oh," I said softly. My wings started to flutter. My parents were hardly ever behind closed doors.

And they never minded when I interrupted them. This was very odd. Was everything okay?

"Don't worry," Chip said. "Maybe they are making plans for the celebration tomorrow night."

I couldn't shake the feeling that something was wrong, very wrong!

7

Sour News

The next morning, Frosting and Taffy were waiting for me in the lemon room.

"Did you talk to your parents about Gobo?" Frosting whispered.

"No," I said. "They were behind

closed doors *all* night. And they left the castle before I woke up."

"That doesn't sound good!" Taffy said.

Just then our music teacher, **Lord Licorice**, flew into the classroom and whispered in Lady Cherry's ear.

"Well, class," Lady Cherry said, "the headmaster just sent a message. We will not be able to see the royal crown jewels today."

The class groaned.

"That isn't fair!" Swirlie said.

"Why not?" Cupcake asked, **pouting**.

Lady Cherry held up her hand for quiet. "We are still planning to go to the Chocolate Museum for our class trip tomorrow instead," she said. "Plans changed for today."

Cupcake turned to face me. "I know there is something sour going on," she whispered. "It must be a troll! I bet the trolls want to steal the crown."

Cupcake was wrong! No troll would steal the royal crown. A troll had given those jewels to the queen, after all.

"What about the Royal Crown Ball?" Swirlie asked.

I thought about my parents behind closed doors. I felt all eyes on me.

Lady Cherry cleared her throat. "I believe all plans are still on for the celebration," she said.

I looked down at my hands. I hoped that was true.

"Everyone, outside," said Lord Licorice. "You have an extra morning recess."

My class flew outside to the playground.

Cupcake and Swirlie started whispering. They came over to Taffy, Frosting, and me with supersour **smirks**.

"I saw guards at the museum last night," Swirlie said.

Cupcake moved over to me. "I bet there was a robbery," she said. "Probably a troll."

"Not all trolls are bad," I hissed.

I stared at Cupcake with an icy-cold look.

"Why are you **defending** trolls?" she asked.

Frosting glared at his sister. "You don't have any proof that a troll took the crown jewels," he said.

"What proof do you need?" Cupcake asked. "Everyone knows trolls steal candy and jewels!" She shook her wings and flew across the yard.

Taffy rolled her eyes. **"Sour**

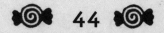

sticks!" she cried. "This isn't good."

"We don't know there was a robbery," I answered. "Lady Cherry didn't say the jewels were stolen."

"And she did say we *were* going to the museum tomorrow," Taffy added.

"But she *didn't* say we were going to see the crown jewels," I said.

"Never believe a **rumor**. Especially if Cupcake is spreading it," Frosting said.

"I hope Gobo hasn't heard this rumor," I whispered.

"We need to ask him," Taffy said. "Let's go after school today."

Frosting agreed. "Plus, I have my old suit to give him for the ball."

Taffy sighed. "If there is a Royal Crown Ball," she said.

8

Rumors

After school, Taffy, Frosting, and I flew to Chocolate Woods. Even though I hadn't spoken to my parents, I was able to get an extra invitation for Gobo.

Gobo was waiting for us when

 47

we arrived. He was pacing back and forth.

"The crown jewels were taken last night!" Gobo cried.

I didn't tell Gobo that Cupcake thought a troll took the crown.

"All the trolls are talking about it," Gobo said. "There were ten guards at the museum last night."

Frosting nodded his head. "I bet," he said. "Who would take the crown?"

Gobo put his hands on his hips. "No matter what stories you have heard, a troll didn't take the crown."

I could see how upset Gobo was about the news. "We know," I answered.

"And I am *not* going to the ball," Gobo said.

"But I have an invitation for you," I said. "This will all be straightened out by tonight."

Gobo shook his head. "There is no place for a troll at a Candy Fairy ball," he said.

I knew Gobo was upset. I didn't blame him.

"Let's go to the castle now," Frosting said. "Mini, this time you have to talk to your parents. You must find out what happened to the jewels."

"Frosting's right!" I said. "Please give us a chance to discover the truth."

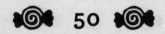

My friends and I raced to Candy Castle, straight to the throne room.

Once again, Chip was standing outside the door.

"Let's ask him if he knows any-thing about the crown jewels," Frosting said.

I guess it wouldn't hurt to ask, I thought.

"Hello, Princess Mini," Chip said, bowing his head.

"Oh, hello," I said. I felt my wings move.

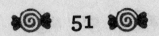

"We were supposed to go on a class trip today to see the royal crown jewels at the Chocolate Museum, but the trip was **canceled**," Taffy said. I was grateful that she spoke up.

"We were wondering about the royal jewels," Frosting said. "Why couldn't we see them today?"

I stepped forward. "We heard a rumor that the crown was missing," I said.

Chip nodded. "The crown was taken last night," he said.

The three of us gasped!

"Oh no!" I exclaimed.

Maybe that was why my parents were behind closed doors. No wonder our trip was canceled! I felt a chill.

Things were bitterer than I had imagined.

9

The Sweetest News

"Did you say that the crown was taken last night?" I asked. I looked up at the tall guard.

"Yes," Chip said. "It was returned to Ice Cream Isles for a cleaning."

A smile spread across my face.

"The crown jewels are being cleaned?" I asked. "The crown was not stolen?"

"Stolen?" the guard cried. "Never!"

"That is the best news!" Taffy exclaimed.

"The queen wanted to have the crown jewels cleaned for the party," Chip said.

I couldn't wait to see Cupcake's face when she heard that the trolls had nothing to do with the missing crown jewels.

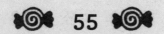

The door to the throne room opened and my parents and grandparents stepped out.

I ran over and gave them all hugs. "I am so happy the royal jewels are safe!" I cried.

"Safe?" my grandmother asked.

"Yes, the jewels are safe!"

"We were so scared the crown was stolen," I said. "We heard the most sour kind of rumor."

"Oh my!" my grandmother exclaimed. "I just wanted to make sure the stones were perfect for

tonight."
Taffy,
Frosting,
and I
explained
the rumor
we had

heard and then told them about
Gobo and Bibi and the jewels.

"He *was* our secret friend," I
explained. "But he has a story to
tell that should be heard by all
Candy Fairies."

"We would love to meet Gobo,"

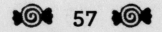

my mother said. "You have been very good friends."

"Would you come with us now to Chocolate Woods?" I asked. "I think if you did, Gobo might change his mind about coming to the ball."

My mother ordered the royal carriage, and we headed to the Chocolate Woods.

When we arrived, I called for Gobo, and he slowly came out of the bushes.

I moved closer to him and held

out my hand. "Come say hello," I told him. "These are my parents and grandparents."

My mother stepped forward. "Hello, Gobo! It is our great

pleasure to meet you," she said.

"Please come to the ball and share your story with Candy Kingdom," my father said.

My grandmother bowed. "You have an important piece of history to tell," she said. "I am **honored** to meet you, Gobo."

Gobo bowed too. "Thank you," he said.

"Will you come tonight?" I asked. I held my breath.

"Yes!" Gobo said, grinning. **"Sure as sugar!"**

10

Royal Crown Ball

The Royal Crown Ball was amazing! The grand room at the Chocolate Museum was decorated in bright rainbow colors, and the royal orchestra played.

My parents invited Lady Cherry

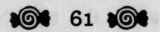

and all the fairies in our class. Everyone was dressed in fancy outfits. My parents and grandparents wore their sparkly best.

At the center of a large room,

there was a large glass case with the royal crown on display.

"Sugar-tastic!" I whispered when I flew in with my parents.

Lady Cherry was the first fairy I saw. She was wearing a long blue dress with a light pink cotton candy wrap.

"Hello, Princess Lolli and Prince Scoop," she said, bowing. "Nice to see you, Princess Mini."

"We are glad you are here to celebrate with us," my mother

replied. She beamed at me and straightened my tiara. "We are so proud that Princess Mini invited Gobo."

"Come with me," my grandmother said as she swooped in and took my hand. "I am about to introduce Gobo."

Together we flew up to the stage. My grandmother stood in the center with a microphone.

"Today we mark the one-hundredth anniversary of the Ice Cream Isles Royal Jewels," she said. "We are so grateful to have a **descendant** of Bibi, the brave troll who gave these jewels to a very wise and kind queen. Please join us, Gobo!"

"Hooray!" cheered the crowd. Gobo looked very nervous waiting by the side of the stage.

I flew to him and took his hand. "I'll be right next to you," I whispered.

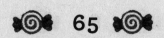

We walked onto the stage and the Candy Fairies continued to clap and cheer.

There was so much joy in the room. Gobo seemed to relax a little bit and waved to the crowd.

"On behalf of all the kingdoms," my grandmother said. "We thank you and honor your great-great-great-grandfather Bibi!"

There was another loud roar.

I saw Frosting and Taffy smiling at us. **Wow!** Even Cupcake and Swirlie were clapping.

"Tonight is perfect," I said to Gobo. "The best part is that you are here with all of us."

"Thank you," Gobo said.

My mother joined us onstage. "Princess Mini, Princess Taffy, and Prince Frosting should be honored as well," my mother said.

She invited the others up

onstage and told us, "You stood by a friend. There is nothing sweeter in this land than friendship."

"Sure as sugar!" I said happily.

The Royal Crown Ball was surely a special night for trolls, Candy Fairies, and new friends in Sugar Valley.

"Now let's dance!" my dad exclaimed.

Word List

canceled (CAN·seld): Called off planning to do something

celebration (SELL·eh·bray·shun): A special event

dangerous (DAIN·juh·rus): Likely to cause harm

defending (dee·FEND·ing): Protecting or taking a side

descendant (dee·SEN·dant): A person who is related to older family members

exhibit (ig·ZIB·it): A display of art or jewels at a museum

honored (ON·ored): Treated someone with respect

huddled (HUH·duld): Gathered close together in a group

interrupted (in·tuh·RUP·ted): Stopped in the middle of something

pouting (POW·ting): Frowning with pushed-out lips

rumor (ROO·mur): A story passed from person to person but not proven to be true

smirks (SMURKS): Unpleasant smiles

spicy (SPY·see): Having a strong, sometimes hot, flavor

stump (STUMP): The part of a tree that is left after the tree has been cut down

vault (VAWLT): A safe, locked place to put jewels or money

Questions

1. What exhibit is at the Chocolate Museum?
2. Why is Gobo's news about his Grandfather Bibi so surprising to Mini?
3. Why doesn't Gobo want to go to the Royal Crown Ball?
4. How does Mini change Gobo's mind?
5. What is bad about spreading rumors?